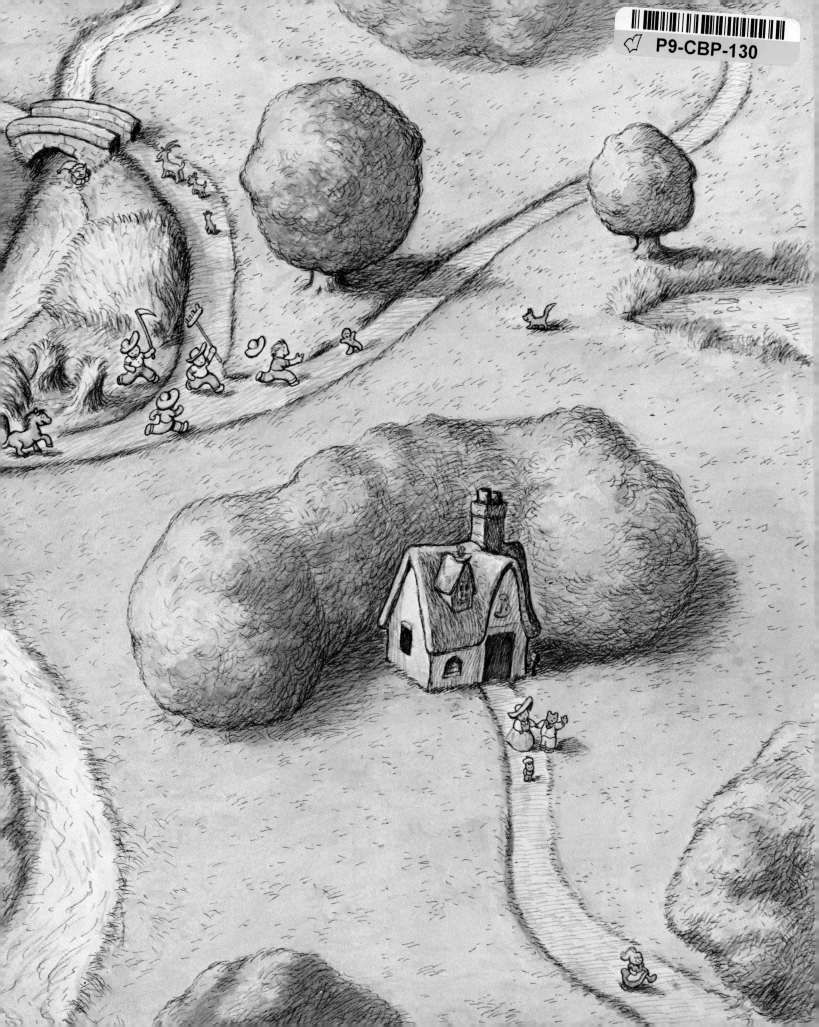

MY FIRST BOOK OF NURSERY TALES

FIVE FAVORITE BEDTIME TALES

retold by
MARIANNA MAYER

illustrated by
WILLIAM JOYCE

RANDOM HOUSE 🏠 NEW YORK

Text copyright © 1983 by Marianna Mayer. Illustrations copyright © 1983 by Random House, Inc. All rights reserved under International and Pan-American Copyright Conventions. Published in the United States by Random House, Inc., New York, and simultaneously in Canada by Random House of Canada Limited, Toronto. *Library of Congress Cataloging in Publication Data*: Mayer, Marianna. My first book of nursery tales. SUMMARY: Retells the well-known tales of Goldilocks and the Three Bears, the Little Red Hen, the Three Billy Goats Gruff, the Three Little Pigs, and the Gingerbread Man. 1. Tales. [1. Folklore] I. Joyce, Bill, ill. II. Title. PZ8.1.M46My 1983 398.2 [E] 82-20452 ISBN: 0-394-85396-2 (trade)
Manufactured in the United States of America   2 3 4 5 6 7 8 9 0

Goldilocks and the Three Bears

Once upon a time there were three bears who lived together in a small house in the woods. There was a great big bear called Papa Bear, a middle-sized bear called Mama Bear, and a tiny little bear called Baby Bear.

They each had a bowl for their porridge—a great big bowl for Papa Bear, a middle-sized bowl for Mama Bear, and a tiny little bowl for Baby Bear.

One sunny morning, after they had made porridge for their breakfast, Mama Bear said, "Let's go for a walk in the woods while we wait for our porridge to cool."

They set out together, leaving their door unlocked, since they were good bears and thought that everyone was good too.

But while they were gone, a little girl who lived on the other side of the woods came along. She was named Goldilocks because her hair was the color of gold. When she saw the pretty little house, she said, "I wonder who lives here?"

First she looked in the window. Next she peeked in the keyhole. And then, seeing that no one was at home, she opened the door and walked right in, for she was not at all a well-brought-up little girl. On the table she saw the three bowls of porridge—the great big bowl, the middle-sized bowl, and the tiny little bowl.

The porridge smelled delicious, so Goldilocks just helped herself to it without waiting to be asked. First she tasted the porridge in the great big bowl.

"Oh, this is too hot," said Goldilocks.

Next she tasted the porridge in the middle-sized bowl.

"Oh, this is too cold," she said.

And then she tasted the porridge in the tiny little bowl.

"Ahh! This is not too hot and not too cold, but just right!" she said, and she ate it all up.

Then Goldilocks looked around the room and saw three chairs—a great big chair, a middle-sized chair, and a tiny little chair. She felt tired from her walk in the woods, so she sat down in the great big chair.

"This chair is too hard," Goldilocks said.

Next she sat in the middle-sized chair.

"This chair is too soft," she said.

Then Goldilocks tried the tiny little chair.

"This chair is not too hard and not too soft, but just right!" she said, and she began to bounce up and down. Suddenly there was a crash and a bang! The tiny little chair broke into pieces and Goldilocks fell to the floor.

She picked herself up, kicked the broken chair, and walked into the bedroom.

It had three beds—a great big bed, a middle-sized bed, and a tiny little bed. As soon as she saw the beds she felt sleepy, so she climbed up onto the great big bed.

"This bed is too hard," Goldilocks said.

Next she tried the middle-sized bed.

"This bed is too soft," she said.

Then she sat down on the tiny little bed.

"This bed is not too hard and not too soft, but just right!" she said. Goldilocks crawled under the covers, without even taking off her shoes, and fell fast asleep.

The three bears soon returned home for their breakfast. Papa Bear looked at his bowl of porridge and began to growl. He saw his spoon standing in the porridge where Goldilocks had carelessly left it.

"SOMEONE'S BEEN TASTING MY PORRIDGE!" Papa Bear growled in his great big rough voice.

Then Mama Bear looked at her bowl and saw her spoon standing in it.

"SOMEONE'S BEEN TASTING MY PORRIDGE!" Mama Bear said in her soft middle-sized voice.

Baby Bear looked at his bowl and saw no porridge at all.

"Someone's been tasting my porridge and has eaten it all up!" Baby Bear cried in his tiny little voice.

Then the three bears looked around the room to see if anything else was missing. Papa Bear saw that the hard cushion on his chair was not in its right place, and he began to roar.

"SOMEONE'S BEEN SITTING IN MY CHAIR!" Papa Bear roared in his great big rough voice.

Mama Bear saw that the soft cushion on her chair was all flattened down.

"SOMEONE'S BEEN SITTING IN MY CHAIR!" Mama Bear said in her soft middle-sized voice.

Then Baby Bear saw his chair and he began to cry.

"Someone's been sitting in my chair and has broken it all up!" cried Baby Bear in his tiny little voice.

Then the three bears went into the bedroom to see if someone was there. Papa Bear saw that the pillow and blanket on his bed were all crumpled, and he began to roar.

"SOMEONE'S BEEN SLEEPING IN MY BED!" Papa Bear roared in his great big rough voice.

Mama Bear saw that her pillow and blanket were flattened down and out of place.

"SOMEONE'S BEEN SLEEPING IN MY BED!" Mama Bear said in her soft middle-sized voice.

Then Baby Bear saw Goldilocks fast asleep in his very own bed.

"Someone's been sleeping in my bed! And here she is!" Baby Bear said in his tiny little voice, which was so sharp and shrill that it awakened Goldilocks.

She opened her eyes, and what did she see but the three bears staring angrily at her.

"GRRRR!" Papa Bear growled in his great big rough voice.

"GRRRR!" Mama Bear growled in her soft middle-sized voice.

"Grrr!" Baby Bear growled in his tiny little voice.

Goldilocks was so frightened that she tumbled out of the bed and ran to the window, and out she jumped. And that was the last the three bears ever saw of that naughty little girl.

The Little Red Hen

There once was a Little Red Hen who, with her chicks, lived on a farm with a Duck, a Cat, and a Pig. The Duck, the Cat, and the Pig were so lazy that the Little Red Hen had to do all the work by herself.

One day the Little Red Hen was scratching in a field for something to eat when she found some grains of wheat.

"This wheat should be planted," she said. "Now who will plant the wheat?"

"Not I," said the Duck.

"Not I," said the Cat.

"Not I," said the Pig.

"Then I will," said the Little Red Hen. And she did.

The grains of wheat grew and grew. When it was tall and yellow, the Little Red Hen said, "The wheat is ripe and ready to be cut. Now who will help cut the wheat?"

"Not I," said the Duck.

"Not I," said the Cat.

"Not I," said the Pig.

"Then I will," said the Little Red Hen. And she did.

When the wheat was cut, the Little Red Hen said, "It's time to thresh the wheat. Now who will beat the grains from the chaff?"

"Not I," said the Duck.

"Not I," said the Cat.

"Not I," said the Pig.

"Then I will," said the Little Red Hen. And she did.

When the wheat was threshed, the Little Red Hen put it into a sack and said, "Now who will take this grain to the mill and have it ground into flour?"

"Not I," said the Duck.

"Not I," said the Cat.

"Not I," said the Pig.

"Then I will," said the Little Red Hen. And she did.

When the Little Red Hen came back from the mill with the sack of flour, she said, "I've planted the wheat. I've cut and threshed it too. I've even carried it to the mill and had it ground into flour. Now who will bake the bread?"

"Not I," said the Duck.

"Not I," said the Cat.

"Not I," said the Pig.

"Then I will," said the Little Red Hen. And she did.

The Duck, the Cat, and the Pig sat in the doorway and watched the Little Red Hen make and bake the bread. Soon the good smell of fresh bread filled the barnyard.

Then the Little Red Hen took the bread out of the oven and said, "Now who will eat the bread?"

"I will!" quacked the Duck.

"I will!" purred the Cat.

"I will!" grunted the Pig.

"Oh, no you won't!" clucked the Little Red Hen, and she called to her chicks. "My chicks and I will eat the bread." And they did.

The Three Billy Goats Gruff

There once were three Billy Goats with the family name Gruff who had eaten all the grass on their mountain. So they set off to find a new mountain covered with sweet grass that would make them grow big and fat.

To get to the new mountain they had to cross a bridge over a river, and under the bridge lived a terrible Troll. He had great big red eyes, a large fat nose, and a huge mouth with long, sharp teeth.

First the littlest Billy Goat Gruff came to the river and started to cross the bridge. *Trip, trap* went his little feet lightly across the bridge.

"Who's that trip-trapping over my bridge?" growled the Troll, and he stuck his ugly face out from under the bridge.

"Oh, it's only I, Little Billy Goat Gruff. I'm going to the mountain to make myself big and fat," said the first Billy Goat Gruff in a tiny voice.

"Oh, no you aren't! I'm going to gobble you up," said the Troll.

"Don't take me! I'm far too little to make a proper meal for you," said the littlest Billy Goat. "Wait just a bit till the second Billy Goat Gruff comes along. He's much bigger."

"Well, be off with you then," snarled the Troll.

Soon the second Billy Goat Gruff came along. TRIP, TRAP! TRIP, TRAP! went his middle-sized feet across the bridge.

"Who's that trip-trapping over my bridge?" shouted the Troll.

"Oh, it's only I, the second Billy Goat Gruff. I'm going to the mountain to make myself fatter," said the second Billy Goat Gruff in a middle-sized voice.

"Oh, no you aren't! I'm going to gobble you up," said the Troll.

"Don't take me! I'm not big enough for you," said the middle-sized Billy Goat Gruff. "Wait for the third Billy Goat Gruff. He will soon be here, and he is much bigger than I am."

"Very well then, be off with you," growled the Troll.

Soon the third Billy Goat Gruff came along. TRIP, TRAP! TRIP, TRAP! TRIP, TRAP! went his big feet across the bridge heavily.

"Who's that trip-trapping over my bridge?" shouted the Troll.

"IT'S I, BILLY GOAT GRUFF. AND WHAT DO *YOU* WANT?" said the Billy Goat Gruff in a very big voice.

"Wait right there, I'm coming to gobble you up!" roared the Troll from beneath the bridge.

"COME UP, THEN. I'M NOT AFRAID OF YOU," said the big Billy Goat Gruff.

The Troll came up, and Billy Goat lowered his head. Then he pointed his big strong horns at the Troll and ran straight at him. What a surprise the Troll got! BUMP! The Troll went flying off the bridge and—SPLASH—into the river, never to be heard of again.

So the three Billy Goats Gruff went to the top of the mountain, where they ate the sweet grass, grew fatter and fatter, and lived happily ever after.

The Gingerbread Man

Once there was an old woman and an old man who lived in an old house all by themselves. They longed for a little boy or girl of their own, and so one day the old woman made a boy out of gingerbread.

She rolled out the dough and cut it in the shape of a little boy. Then she gave him two raisins for eyes, a mouth of pink frosting, and candy buttons down the front of his jacket.

"Now we'll have our own little boy," she said, and she popped him into the hot oven.

When it was time for the Gingerbread Boy to be done, she opened the oven door. But before she could take out the pan, the Gingerbread Boy sat up and jumped right out of the oven! He ran across the kitchen, out the door, along the garden path, and down the road just as fast as his gingerbread legs could carry him. The old woman and the old man could hardly believe their eyes.

"Stop! Stop, little Gingerbread Boy!" called the old woman and the old man, and they ran after him. But the Gingerbread Boy only looked back and laughed.

"Run! Run! Run! Catch me if you can. You can't get me! I'm the Gingerbread Man, I am, I am!"

And they couldn't catch him.

The Gingerbread Boy ran on and on. Soon he came to a cow eating grass by the roadside.

"Stop, little Gingerbread Boy! You smell delicious," said the cow. But the Gingerbread Boy laughed and said:

"I've run away from the old woman and the old man,
And I can run away from you, I can, I can!"

So the cow ran after him, and the Gingerbread Boy shouted:

"Run! Run! Run! Catch me if you can.
You can't get me! I'm the Gingerbread Man,
I am, I am!"

And the cow couldn't catch him.

So the Gingerbread Boy ran on and on. Soon he came to a horse standing in a meadow.

"Please stop, Gingerbread Boy! You look so good to eat," said the horse. But the Gingerbread Boy did not stop running. He laughed and called back to the horse:

"I've run away from the old woman and the old man,
I've run away from the cow,
And I can run away from you, I can, I can!"

So the horse ran after him, and the Gingerbread Boy ran faster and faster, calling out:

"Run! Run! Run!
Catch me if you can.
You can't get me!
I'm the Gingerbread Man,
I am, I am!"

And the horse couldn't catch him.

The Gingerbread Boy ran and ran, down the road, past a barn, and near a field of mowers. When the mowers saw the tasty-looking Gingerbread Boy run by, they stopped their work and ran after him.

"Wait, wait, Gingerbread Boy! You were made to eat," said the mowers. But the Gingerbread Boy did not wait for the mowers. He laughed louder than ever and called out:

"I've run away from
the old woman and the old man,
I've run away from the cow,
I've run away from the horse,
And I can run away from you,
I can, I can!"

And, try as they did, the mowers couldn't catch him.

Now the Gingerbread Boy was very proud of himself. He was sure no one could ever catch him. So when he saw a fox running through the woods, the Gingerbread Boy called out:

"Run! Run! Run! Catch me if you can.
You can't get me! I'm the Gingerbread Man,
I am, I am!
I've run away from the old woman and the old man,
I've run away from the cow,
I've run away from the horse,
I've run away from the mowers,
And I can run away from you, I can, I can!"

"Why, I'm sure you can," said the fox politely. "But I wouldn't dream of catching you even if I could."

Just then the Gingerbread Boy came to a river. He knew at once that he would have to cross the river to get away from the old woman and the old man, the cow, the horse, and all the mowers who were still running after him. But he was afraid to jump in, for he could not swim.

"Here, jump on my tail and I will take you across," said the fox.

So the Gingerbread Boy jumped onto the fox's tail, and the fox swam into the river.

Soon the fox said, "You are too heavy on my tail, Gingerbread Boy. I am afraid I will get you wet. Jump up on my back." And the Gingerbread Boy jumped onto the fox's back.

After swimming a little farther, the fox said, "Oh dear, the water is much deeper here. You must jump up on my nose, Gingerbread Boy, or you will surely get wet." And the Gingerbread Boy jumped onto the fox's nose.

Then the fox threw back his head and—snip, snap—ate the Gingerbread Boy in one big gulp. The fox licked his lips happily as he reached the shore. And the Gingerbread Boy was never seen or heard of again.

The Three Little Pigs

There once were three little pigs who, when they were old enough, left their mother's home to set out on their own.

"I'm going to build myself a house of straw," said the first little pig. And he did just that.

"I will build my house of sticks," said the second little pig. And he did just that.

"Oh, I want a house that is solid and strong," said the third little pig. "I'll build my house of bricks." And he did just that.

One day a hungry wolf came to the door of the first little pig's house of straw. "Little pig, little pig, let me come in," said the wolf.

The first little pig answered, "No, no, no! Not by the hair of my chinny, chin, chin."

"Then I'll huff and I'll puff and I'll blow your house in," said the wolf.

The wolf huffed and he puffed and he blew the house down. The little pig got blown right out of his house. But he ran to his brother's house of sticks and got safely inside before the wolf came knocking.

"Little pigs, little pigs, let me come in," said the wolf.

The second little pig answered, "No, no, no! Not by the hair of my chinny, chin, chin."

"Then I'll huff and I'll puff and I'll blow your house in," said the wolf.

So the wolf huffed and he puffed and he puffed and he huffed and he blew the house down. But the two little pigs ran away and got to their brother's house of bricks just in time.

Then the wolf knocked at the door of the third little pig's house of bricks. The first and second little pigs were so frightened that they hid under the bed.

"Little pigs, little pigs, let me come in," said the wolf.

The third little pig called, "No, no, no! Not by the hair of my chinny, chin, chin."

"Then I'll huff and I'll puff and I'll blow your house in," said the wolf.

So the wolf huffed and he puffed and he puffed and he huffed and he puffed, but he could not blow the little brick house down.

The wolf kept thinking how delicious the little pig would be, and soon he thought of a trick to get the little pig to come out of his house.

"Little pig, I know of a nice patch of turnips in Mr. Smith's garden," said the wolf sweetly. "If you'll come with me tomorrow morning I'll show you, and we can gather them together."

"All right," said the third little pig. "What time will you come?"

"At six o'clock," said the wolf.

The first and second little pigs were too afraid to go, but the third little pig had a plan. He went to the turnip patch the moment the sun came up, gathered the turnips, and returned to his brick house before the wolf came knocking at his door.

"It's six o'clock, little pig. Are you ready?" called the wolf.

"Ready! I've been and come back and have a nice basket of turnips for lunch," said the little pig.

The wolf was angry, but he was more determined than ever to catch the little pig, and he quickly thought of another trick.

"Well, then would you like to go apple picking with me?" asked the wolf.

"Where?" asked the little pig.

"There is a fine apple tree in Farmer Brown's orchard. I'll come for you tomorrow morning at five o'clock," said the wolf.

The next morning, before the sun even came up, the third little pig hurried to Farmer Brown's orchard. He had to climb the tree to get the best apples, and he was just about to come down when he saw the wolf coming.

"I see you got here early. Are they nice apples?" asked the wolf.

"Yes, indeed. Here, try one," said the little pig, and he threw an apple all the way to the other side of the orchard. While the wolf went to get it, the little pig jumped from the tree and ran quickly home.

The next day the wolf came and said to the third little pig, "There is a fair in town today. Shall we go together?"

"Oh, yes," said the little pig. "When do you want to go?"

"At four o'clock," said the wolf.

So, of course, the little pig went to the fair by himself very early that afternoon. At the fair he bought a butter churn, which he was carrying home when he saw the wolf coming up the hill.

Now the little pig was really frightened. There was nowhere to hide—except inside the butter churn. No sooner had the little pig climbed into the churn than it tipped over and began to roll bumpity-bump down the hill.

Faster and faster it went, straight for the wolf. The wolf was so frightened that he jumped out of its way and ran home.

Later the wolf went to the little pig's house and said, "On my way to the fair a great big round thing chased me down the hill. I was so frightened that I never went to the fair."

The little pig laughed and laughed. "So I frightened you, did I!" said the little pig. "*I* was in that great big round thing. It was a butter churn that I bought at the fair."

Now the wolf was so angry that he began to growl. "Oh, you won't get away from me this time. I'm coming down your chimney, and I shall eat you and your brothers at last."

The first and second little pigs rushed into the cupboard to hide. But the third little pig went to the fireplace and quickly took the lid off the big pot of water that was boiling there.

The wolf came tumbling down the chimney and fell—SPLASH!—right into the boiling water. What a howl the wolf made! Out he jumped from the pot and ran from the house.

And the three little pigs lived happily ever after,
for the wolf never troubled them again.